F
LEV

Levine, Gail Carson.

The fairy's return.

452663

$14.89

The Fairy's Return

The Princess Tales

The Fairy's Return

Gail Carson Levine

ILLUSTRATED BY Mark Elliott

HarperCollins*Publishers*

The Fairy's Return

Text copyright © 2002 by Gail Carson Levine

Illustrations copyright © 2002 by Mark Elliott

Printed in the United States of America. All rights reserved.

www.harperchildrens.com

Library of Congress Cataloging-in-Publication Data

Levine, Gail Carson.

The fairy's return / Gail Carson Levine ; illustrated by Mark Elliott.

p.   cm.

"Princess tales."

Summary: In a retelling of the Grimm Brothers' "The Golden Goose," the good-natured son of a baker wins the heart of a princess, with the help of a fairy and a magic goose.

ISBN 0-06-623800-5 — ISBN 0-06-623801-3 (lib. bdg.)

[1. Fairy tales. 2. Folklore—Germany.] I. Elliott, Mark, ill. II. Title.

PZ8.L4793 Fal 2002   2002001681

398.2'0943—dc21   CIP

                                        AC

Typography by Michele Tupper

1   2   3   4   5   6   7   8   9   10

❖

First Edition

Love to Betsy and Ben and Amy and
Sean and their animal pals

—G.C.L.

BOOKS BY
Gail Carson Levine

Ella Enchanted
Dave at Night
The Wish
The Two Princesses of Bamarre

THE PRINCESS TALES:

The Fairy's Mistake
The Princess Test
Princess Sonora and the Long Sleep
Cinderellis and the Glass Hill
For Biddle's Sake

Betsy Who Cried Wolf

One

Once upon a time in the kingdom of Biddle a baker's son and a princess fell in love. This is how it came about—

Robin, the baker's son, rode to Biddle Castle in the back of the bakery cart. His older brothers, Nat and Matt, sat on the driver's bench with their father, Jake, who was a poet as well as a baker.

Robin began a joke. "What's a dwarf's—"

"Son," Jake said,

"A joker is a fool,
Who never went to a place of
learning."

Nat said, "Jokers are dottydaftish." He had a knack for inventing words.

Matt said, "Jokes are dumdopety." He had a knack for inventing words too.

Robin hated being thought stupid. "Jokes aren't dumb or dopey, and I'm not dotty or daft. If you'd ever listen to a whole joke, you'd see." If they did, they'd realize that jokers were just as smart as poets and word inventors.

Jake just shook his head. Robin was the first moron in family history. Not only did he make up jokes, he also gave things away. Why only a week ago, on the lad's eleventh birthday to be exact, Robin had given a roll to a beggar. For free!

Generosity was against family policy. Jake had told his sons repeatedly never to give anyone something for nothing. He had learned this from his own father, a genius who could make up three poems at once.

The bakery cart rumbled across the Biddle Castle drawbridge. At the door to the Royal Kitchen, Jake reined in their nag, Horsteed, who had been named by Nat.

When all the bread had been carried into the kitchen, Jake began to chat with the Royal Chief Cook. As Jake often said,

> *"A nice customer chat*
> *Puts a coin in your bonnet."*

Nat chatted with the Royal First Assistant Cook, and Matt chatted with the Royal Second Assistant Cook.

Robin began to tell his dwarf joke to the Royal Third Assistant Cook, but the Royal Third Assistant Cook interrupted with his recipe for pickled goose feet with jellied turnips.

Robin disliked jellied anything, so after he'd heard the recipe three times, he said, "How interesting. Please excuse me." He slipped out the Royal Kitchen Door and into the Royal Garden, where commoners weren't allowed.

But he didn't know that.

Two

𝒟ame Cloris, the Royal Governess, sat primly upright on a bench in a small meadow in the garden. Her lace cap had slipped over her face, and it fluttered as she breathed. She was fast asleep.

Princess Lark sat on the grass nearby, her favorite ball a few feet away. She wished she had someone to play with.

Yesterday had been her eleventh birthday, and her birthday party had been awful, just like every other party she'd ever had. The guests had been children of the castle nobility, and the party had begun with a game of hide-and-seek. Lark had taken the first turn as It. While she counted, she wished with all her might that this time her guests would really play with her.

But when she opened her eyes, she saw that no one had hidden. Oh, they were pretending to hide. Aldrich, the Earl of Pildenue's son, was standing next to a tree, with one foot concealed behind it. And his sister, Cornelia, had stationed herself behind a bush that only came up to her waist.

The children wouldn't hide because they were afraid Lark would fail to find them. And not one of them dared to let a princess fail at anything.

She had told them she wouldn't mind. She had also said she wouldn't mind being It forever. But it didn't matter what she said.

The next activity, baseball, was even worse. When Lark was at bat, if she hit the ball at all—a yard, a foot, half an inch—no one tried to catch it. They thought it would be disrespectful to make a princess out, so Lark had to dash around the bases for a home run she hadn't earned.

When the other team was at bat, they tried not to hit the ball, because it would never do for their team to beat Lark's.

Lark declared the game over after one inning and declared the party over too. She ate her birthday cake alone—the single bite she was able to get down before she ran to her room, sobbing.

And now here she was, in the garden with her ball and a sleeping governess. She watched idly as Robin approached. She noticed that his jerkin was plain brown, without even the tiniest jewel. How unusual. And there was a hole in his breeches.

She sat up straight. His feet were bare. He was a commoner!

Lark had never spoken to a commoner. Maybe he'd be different.

Robin had no idea who the old lady and the lass were. He only knew the lass looked sad. Maybe a joke would cheer her up, if she'd let him tell it.

"Hello," he said. "What's a dwarf's . . ." She wasn't interrupting. He began to feel nervous. ". . . favorite food?"

She smiled up at him. He hadn't bowed, which was wonderful. But she had no idea what the answer was. The king of the dwarfs had visited Biddle last year, but she couldn't remember what he'd eaten. "Potatoes?"

Robin's heart started to pound. She was going to listen to the punch line! "No. Strawberry shortcake." He waited.

"Why straw—" Then she knew. She started laughing. A dwarf! Strawberry *short*cake!

Robin laughed too, for sheer delight.

She liked the joke! He sat down next to her and tried another one. "Which rank of nobility is best at math?"

Was this another joke? "The earl?"

"No. He's earl-y and catches the worm."

She pictured Aldrich's father grubbing for worms. That was so funny.

Robin thought she had the best laugh, gurgly and tinkly. "It's the count."

Numbers! A count! She laughed harder.

Robin thought, She has a superb sense of humor.

Dame Cloris, the governess, snored, a long rattle followed by two snorts. Robin and Lark giggled.

"Why is a king like a yardstick?"

Lark tried to guess. Her father didn't look anything like a yardstick, not with his bad posture. She gave up and shrugged.

9

"They're both rulers."

She laughed. Rulers! The king would love it. "I can't wait to tell Father."

Robin frowned. "You're lucky. My father hates jokes. Is your father a Royal Servant?"

He didn't know? Oh, no! As soon as she told him, he'd turn stiff and uncomfortable, just like everybody else. She thought of lying, but she didn't like to lie, and he was too nice to lie to anyway. "No. He's the king."

He blinked. "Then you're—"

She nodded. "I'm Princess Lark."

Three

Robin jumped up and bowed. A princess liked his jokes! Bowing wasn't enough. He took her hand and pumped it up and down.

Lark was delighted. Most people were afraid to touch her. "What's your name?"

"Robin."

"We both have bird names!" It was amazing.

"I wouldn't like to be named Spoonbill." He grinned. "Or Swallow. Good morning, Master Swallow. How did your breakfast go down?"

"Or my name could be Vulture. Good

morning, Princess Vulture. I hate to think what you had for breakfast." She stood up. "Why doesn't your father like your jokes?"

"I don't know why."

He looks sad, Lark thought. "They're terrific jokes. How do you think of them?"

"I don't know." He blushed. "I just do."

"All the time?"

"Except when I'm unhappy or angry. Then I can't make up any. I can't even remember my old ones." He changed the subject. He didn't like to think about being jokeless. "Why is a bakery—"

Dame Cloris moaned in her sleep.

"Who's she?"

"She's Dame Cloris, my governess." Lark giggled. "She's a deep sleeper. Why is a bakery what?"

"Oh. Why is a bakery like a garden?"

Lark tried to figure it out. One was outdoors and one was indoors. That wasn't it. She stopped trying. It was more fun to let him surprise her. "I give up."

"They're both flowery." Or floury, he thought.

She chuckled. "You're clever."

That wasn't what his father and brothers thought. "My father's a baker. You should visit our bakery. It's in Snettering-on-Snoakes. You could come tomorrow." If she came, he wouldn't have to wait a week to see her again. "Or the next day." And maybe she'd make Jake and Nat and Matt listen to a joke.

"I'd like to come."

"When you do, could you order me to tell you a joke, a whole one, all the way through?"

She nodded. Nobody had ever asked

for her help before. They just wanted to do things for her.

Robin could hardly wait. Everything would change when his family heard a whole joke. He loved Lark!

He was so happy, he had to do something. He picked up her ball and gave it to her. "Want to play catch?"

Did she! She threw him the ball. He threw it back. He threw hard. He didn't seem to care if she failed to catch it. This was what she'd always wanted. This was heavenly.

She terrible at catch, since she'd never had a chance to practice. But she was happy to chase the ball and throw it back as well as she could.

Sometimes when she missed the ball, it wasn't her fault, though. He kept telling jokes and timing them so that she was laughing when he threw the ball. He was playing tricks to *make* her miss. She loved him!

The ball bounced off her arm. She and Robin ran after it, but—

Oh no! It hit Dame Cloris's skirts, right below the knee.

Dame Cloris yelped and opened her eyes. A commoner! With Princess Lark! She screamed, and then she fainted.

Lark and Robin rushed to her. Two Royal Garden Guards came on the run. One waved smelling salts under Dame Cloris's nose. The other picked Robin up by his collar and carried him away.

Robin yelled, "Don't forget! Come to the bakery."

"I'll be there."

The guard dumped Robin at the Royal Kitchen Door. "Stay out of the garden," he growled, and marched off. Robin slipped into the kitchen, where Jake and Nat and Matt were ending their customer chats.

"A COMMONER! WITH PRINCESS LARK!"

On the way back to Snettering-on-Snoakes Robin announced, "While you were talking, I played catch with Princess Lark, and—"

"You falsfibbulator!" Nat started laughing. "That's the sillfooliest thing I ever heard!"

Matt laughed too. "It's nutcrazical!"

Jake stopped the cart. "Mat! Natt! I mean Nat! Matt! Don't make fun of Robin just because he isn't as brilliant as we are. He only *wishes* he could meet a princess and play—"

"I don't only—"

"But it's a bad wish." Jake was proud to be a commoner and wouldn't have wanted to play catch with a king.

*"Royalty and commoners must never mix.
Remember this, or you will be in a predicament."*

"She's going to come to the bakery."
So there.

Jake was shocked. Robin truly believed he'd met the princess. He was too stupid to know what was real and what wasn't. He was an imbecile.

Robin repeated, "She's coming. And she likes my jokes. You'll see."

Four

In the Royal Dining Hall that evening, Lark said, "Father . . ."

"Harrumph?"

"Today I played with the lad I want to marry someday." She laughed, remembering the ruler joke.

The king smiled. His daughter had a lovely laugh, and he didn't hear it often enough. "Well, harrumph?" Meaning, *Well, who?* King Humphrey V was known far and wide as King Harrumphrey.

"He's Robin, the baker's son. He told—"

King Harrumphrey's face turned red.

"You're not harrumphying any har-
rumpher's son!"

"I will so harrumphy him, I mean,
marry him!"

"Harrumph!"

The next morning Lark told Dame
Cloris that she wanted to go to
Snettering-on-Snoakes.

Dame Cloris yawned. "I'm feeling too
sleepy, Your Highness. I can't go with
you . . . and you can't go without me."

The following day Dame Cloris said
she was still too sleepy. The day after
that she was too tired, and the next day
she was too sleepy again.

Lark appealed to her father. "It would
be educational for me," she said. "I'd
meet our subjects."

King Harrumphrey frowned. Was the
baker's son behind this? "You don't have
to meet any harrumphs. When the Royal

Chief Councillor puts our golden harrumph on your head someday, you'll
harrumph all you need in an instant."

"But Father, what if I don't harru—
know all I need?"

"Sweetharrumph, trust us, commoners are harrumph. Even worse, they're
harrumph."

"Please, can't I go? I won't stay long."

"No, you can't. Not for all the harrumph in Kulornia."

⚓ ⚓ ⚓

Robin was miserable when Lark didn't
come to the bakery the next day or the
next. He couldn't even cheer himself
up with jokes, because he was too upset
to think of any. And it didn't help that
Nat kept calling him His Hikingness,
and that Matt kept saying, "Where's
your prinroycess?"

It crossed Robin's mind that Lark had only pretended to like his jokes. After all, nobody else liked them.

But she *had* liked them. He was sure of it. And she had liked him. He couldn't have imagined it.

Maybe she'd hurt herself and couldn't come. Or maybe that snooty Dame wouldn't let her come. That must have been it. He felt better and made up three jokes.

The next time they delivered bread, he'd find out what had happened. He'd tell the new jokes, and he'd get proof that they'd met. Maybe she'd write on Royal Stationery that she thought he was clever and his jokes were funny.

Most important of all, when he saw her, he'd tell her he loved her.

But Jake wouldn't take him to the castle anymore. He said,

"To the castle you could come
If you weren't so darn moronic."

That made Robin mad. He wasn't moronic! And if his father wouldn't take him, he'd go on his own.

Every afternoon one of the brothers went to Snoakes Forest to chop wood for the bakery oven. Whoever it was packed a picnic lunch, took the family's ax, and set off.

When it was his turn, Robin chopped the wood as fast as he could. Then he hiked past the Sleep In Inn, through fields and low hills, and on to Biddle Castle.

On the way he thought of a dozen more jokes. The seventh was his favorite: Why do noblemen like to stare? Because they're peers.

He pictured Lark's reaction. First

surprise, and then her musical laugh, which would make him feel prouder than a prince and smarter than anyone in his whole family tree.

But when Robin reached the castle, he couldn't get past the Royal Drawbridge Guard.

He tried again on his next seven turns chopping wood. Sometimes the Royal Drawbridge Guard stopped him. He got past that guard a few times, only to be stopped by the Royal Castle Door Guard or the Royal Garden Gate Guard. Once, he managed to enter the castle, but the moment he put his foot on the Royal Grand Staircase, the Royal Grand Staircase Guard rushed at him and tossed him out as if he were a sack of flour.

Oh, Lark! Oh, love! He might never see her again, the one person in Biddle who appreciated a good joke.

Five

Two years passed, but Lark didn't forget Robin. How could she, when he was the only one who'd ever treated her as a normal person? How could she, when the last time she'd laughed had been with him?

King Harrumphrey tried to make her laugh. He'd sneak up on her and tickle her. But she'd stopped being ticklish long ago. He'd make funny faces. They might have made her laugh, if it hadn't been his fault she couldn't visit Robin. So she'd scowl instead.

The king often sent the Royal Jester

to amuse her. But the jester was as afraid
of offending her as everybody else. So
he'd just turn cartwheels and never tell
jokes. And his cartwheels weren't that
funny.

⚓ ⚓ ⚓

Two more years passed. Nat became
betrothed to Holly, the oldest of the
Sleep In innkeeper's three daughters.
Matt became betrothed to the middle sister, Molly.

Robin had stopped thinking of Lark a
hundred times a day. Whenever he did
remember her, he concentrated on something else to keep from feeling bad.

He still hadn't succeeded in telling his
family a complete joke. He would have
given up, but jokes are meant to be told,
and they'd pop out in spite of himself.

And he still hadn't convinced his

family that he wasn't simpleminded. One day, in desperation, he gave in and tried word inventing. He said, "I may not be brillbrainiant, but I'm smarquick enough."

But Nat said, "Stupidated people always think they're keenwittish."

And Matt said, "Your words are the flimflawsiest I've ever heard."

Jake, however, thought Robin's invented words were a good sign. He began to hope that his youngest boy was finally catching up to the rest of the family.

That is, until the day Robin gave an entire muffin to the tailor. Robin was at the front of the bakery, taking coins and making change from the cash box. The tailor, who was the poorest person in Snettering-on-Snoakes, stepped forward with a halfpenny for the leg of a gingerbread man. Robin saw him look

27

hungrily at a blueberry muffin.

Robin glanced around. Nat was taking scones out of the oven. Matt was in the storeroom. And Jake was looking down as he rolled out dough.

Robin grabbed a blueberry muffin just as Jake raised his head. The baker watched, appalled, as Robin passed the muffin to the tailor.

"Stop!" Jake shouted.

The tailor ran out of the shop.

Jake's hopes for Robin collapsed. The lad didn't understand proper behavior. Jake repeated his rule slowly.

"Never ever give anything away
  for free,
  As my father said. Listen to him
  and to I."

From then on Jake wouldn't let Robin do anything except knead dough, the

"'STOP!' JAKE SHOUTED."

most boring job in the bakery. Robin hated it, and he despaired of ever proving he wasn't thickheaded.

A week later Golly, the youngest of the innkeeper's daughters, sat herself down on the bench next to Robin's kneading table. She said, "Dearie, I fear you're worrying about me."

Why? he wondered. Was something wrong with her? She looked healthy.

"You're fretting that I won't marry you."

He stopped kneading.

She went on. "Some wenches may not want a stupid husband, dearie, but I do. I'm bossy, so when we're wed, I'll run the Sleep In and I'll run you."

Robin gulped. "I'm not marrying anybody." Lark flashed into his mind. Once he would have liked to marry her.

Golly poked his arm and laughed. "At

the inn, your job will be fluffing up the
pillows. That's like kneading, dearie."

Jake left his cake batter and came to
them.

> "Son, Golly will make a fine wife,
>   Since your mind's not sharp as a
>   dagger."

"I'm not marrying anybody."
Jake laughed along with Golly.

Six

Golly sat with Robin all morning, and she didn't stop talking for a second. She told him who would be invited to their wedding and which songs would be sung and which dances danced. She told him what jerkin to wear on the wedding day and which side to part his hair on.

He didn't knead the dough that morning. He punched it and squashed it and strangled it.

Eventually Golly left to have her lunch at the inn. Robin packed his own lunch in a basket and left too. It was his turn to chop wood, but first he needed to walk off the hours with Golly. He circled around the Sleep In so she wouldn't see him and headed for the hills and fields south of Biddle Castle.

He wasn't far from the castle when he heard someone singing in the distance. He stood still. He'd heard that voice before. He heard a deeper sound. It was familiar too. He ran toward the sounds.

When he got closer, he could hear the words to the song.

> *"O alas. O alack.*
> *O woe is me.*
> *I've lost my true love,*
> *And I'll never fly free."*

As he ran, he thought, That's odd. *Me* rhymes with *free*.

Almost a mile from Robin, Lark was sitting on the bank of Snoakes Stream.

She'd pulled her skirts up to her knees and had taken off her slippers and her hose. Her feet dangled in the stream. She was feeding the ducks and singing her heart out.

> *"My love's not a widgeon,*
> *Nor a pigeon."*

Those are birds! Robin thought. He ran faster.

> *"My love's not a macaw,*
> *Nor a jackdaw."*

The voice was farther away than he'd thought. He was getting near the castle.

> *"My love's not a waterfowl,*
> *Nor a tawny owl.*
> *O alas. O alack.*

O woe is me.
I've lost my Robin . . ."

A robin! Me? He was out of breath, but he managed one last burst of speed.

There they were. An elderly lady with a lace cap over her face was snoring on a blanket. And Lark was on the stream bank.

"And we'll never fly free."

He rushed to her. "Lark!"

She turned. "Robin?" She stood, almost losing her footing on the slippery stones in the stream. Her skirts trailed in the water. She smiled radiantly. "Robin!"

He thought of a joke. "What does the postal coach driver wear in cold weather?"

A joke! Lark hadn't felt so happy in years. "I don't know. What?"

He'd missed her so. He hadn't realized how much till now. He forgot about the joke and just smiled at her.

Dame Cloris stirred on the blanket. In her dream King Harrumphrey was making her a countess.

Lark prompted Robin. "What?"

What what? Oh, the joke. "When it's cold out, the postal coach driver wears a coat of mail."

She thought for a second, then laughed. A coat of mail! A coat of letters!

He'd never stopped loving her, not for a minute, whether he'd known it or not.

She began to climb out of the stream, but she lost her balance. "Oh, no!" She reached out to Robin. Before he could grab her, she fell backward into the water with a big splash.

In the governess's dream, the king's

sword clanged. He touched it to her forehead. "I harrumph you a Royal Harrumphess."

Robin thought Lark might be hurt. He waded in. She laughed and splashed him.

He splashed her back. She was delighted. No one else would have splashed her. She held out her hands as if she wanted him to help her up, but when he took them, she pulled him down.

Water got in his nose. He snorted and shook the hair out of his eyes. He splashed Lark again.

She laughed.

Dame Cloris's snore changed pitch. She dreamed there was a commotion at the door of the Royal Throne Room.

Lark brushed the water out of her eyes. "I missed you," she said. "I tried to go to your bakery, but nobody would let me."

She did try! "I went to the castle to find you."

"You did?"

Dame Cloris whimpered. In her dream, seven commoners strode into the throne room.

Robin said, "But I couldn't get to you. The guards kept stopping me." He took a deep breath. "I love you."

"I love you. Will you marry me?"

Robin knelt in the water. "Yes, I'll marry you. I'm honored. I'm . . ." He leaned over to kiss her hand.

In the dream the commoners chanted, "No countesses for governesses! No governesses for countesses!" Dame Cloris woke up. She opened her eyes and saw Lark and Robin in the water. She screamed.

Seven

A Royal Drawbridge Guard, his sword drawn, raced to Dame Cloris's aid.

Robin surged out of the stream and ran, calling behind him, "I love you."

Lark called back, "I love you. Remember, we're betrothed."

Dame Cloris fainted. The guard picked her up along with Lark's slippers and hose. He escorted Lark to the Royal Throne Room, where she stood in her bare feet, dripping on the Royal Tile Floor. He placed Dame Cloris on a chair. She revived and told the king what she'd witnessed.

King Harrumphrey yelled *"Harrumph!"* for a full five minutes. Lark just looked defiant.

Finally, his anger collapsed. "Larkie, why do you want to harrumphy him?"

"He makes me laugh." And he treated her like she was an ordinary person. And she loved to be with him.

The king thought about it. There was nothing wrong with laughter. But laughing with a commoner was vulgar. Laughing with a prince was excellent.

Hmm . . . He summoned the Royal Chief Scribe.

"We wish to harrumph a proclamation."

The scribe unrolled a scroll and dipped her pen in ink.

"Hear harrumph. Hear harrumph."

Hear ye. Hear ye, the scribe wrote.

"Insofar and inasharrumph that we

have a harrumphter . . ."

Insofar and inasmuch as we have a scepter . . .

"Not this harrumphter." The king raised his scepter. "That harrumphter." He pointed at Lark.

. . . daughter . . .

King Harrumphrey continued.

Lark listened, horror-struck.

"And said harrumphter, Princess Harrumph, is old harrumph to marry—"

"Father!"

He ignored her and went on.

The scribe wrote, *. . . and said daughter, Princess Lark, is old enough to marry, then let it be known that we will bestow her hand upon any . . .* She was stuck again. She thought for a moment and wrote, *. . . man who . . . .*

King Harrumphrey tapped the scroll. "Not that 'any harrumph.'"

The scribe wrote *noble* in tiny letters to the left of *man*.

The king was getting annoyed. "Not 'any harrumphman.' 'Any harrumph.'"

"He means 'any baker's son,'" Lark said.

King Harrumphrey frowned, and the scribe knew better than to write *baker's son*.

The king roared, "Harrumph! Any prince who can make said princess harrumph."

. . . *any prince who can make said princess harrumph*. The scribe crossed out *harrumph*. Happy! Must be. She wrote, *happy.*

"Not 'harrumphy.'" King Harrumphrey paused. He wanted Lark to be happy. And she would be. The proclamation would make sure of it. "Not 'harrumphy.' 'Harrumph.'"

"THE KING ROARED, 'HARRUMPH!'"

In turn the scribe tried *wise, good at checkers, able to speak six languages, say harrumph more often, live a long time.* The scroll was getting messy, and she was going to have to copy it all over, if she ever figured out what it was supposed to say.

At last, the king shook his belly and said, "Har har har harrumph."

She got it.

Hear ye. Hear ye. Insofar and inasmuch as we have a daughter, and said daughter, Princess Lark, is old enough to marry, then let it be known that we will bestow her hand upon any prince who can make said princess laugh.

⚓ ⚓ ⚓

After he finished chopping wood, Robin returned to the bakery and started kneading again. He felt so joyful that new jokes were coming to him as fast as he could think.

Nat said, "Father has splenthrillous news, Robin."

Today's a good day for good news, Robin thought, smiling.

Jake cleared his throat and announced that Nat, Matt, and Robin would wed Holly, Molly, and Golly in two weeks. He added, "From then on,

"Nat and Matt will roll dough for the
    pie tin,
While Robin fluffs up pillows at the
    hotel."

Robin's jokes stopped coming, and he almost screamed. Golly was the last person he wanted for a wife. She didn't have a bit of Lark's sweetness, Lark's sense of humor, Lark's complete lovableness.

He took a deep breath. He was going to marry Lark. She'd tell her father about their betrothal, and then she'd come to him or send for him, or whatever royalty would do.

But what if the king didn't want him to marry her?

Well, maybe he wouldn't at first. But she'd persuade him. She'd tell him how much they loved each other. He'd understand.

Eight

Lark couldn't sleep all night. What if a real prince made her laugh? What if he told a joke almost as good as one of Robin's, and she laughed before she caught herself? She wouldn't love the prince, but she'd be stuck with him.

She worried about it till dawn. Finally she decided that she had to make herself sad, so sad there'd be no chance of a laugh, no matter what any ridiculous prince said.

While she dressed, she thought of the calamities that befell people every day. They stubbed their toes, lost their favorite hat feathers, put spoiled raspberries into their mouths, were stung by bees, misspelled words, dropped their candy in the dirt. The list was endless.

A tear trickled down her cheek.

While she waited for the first prince to come, she read tragedies in the Royal Library. Within a few days she was weeping steadily. She cried herself to sleep at night and woke up crying in the morning.

King Harrumphrey hated to see her cry. It made him feel like crying too. He would have done almost anything to make his Larkie happy. Anything but let her marry a commoner.

A week before Robin's wedding to Golly, the first prince arrived at Biddle Castle. He was taken to the Royal Tournament Arena to perform before an audience of Lark, King Harrumphrey, Dame Cloris, the Royal Councillors, and any Royal Nobles who wanted to come. No commoners allowed.

The prince juggled cheeses while a mouse stood on his head. The councillors and the courtiers and the king laughed and slapped their knees. Lark wept.

In the next five days, more princes came and performed. A prince told shepherd jokes. His best joke was *Why is a bandit like a shepherd's staff?* The punch line was *They're both crooks*. The audience hooted with laughter. Lark rolled her eyes and wished for Robin. Then she wept.

A prince talked to his foot and pretended it was answering him. Lark recited under her breath, "Suffering, tribulation, death, drought, plague . . ." She wept.

After each performance she asked for

"The prince juggled cheeses while a mouse stood on his head."

permission to marry Robin, but the king always harrumphed no.

⚓ ⚓ ⚓

Two days remained before the wedding. Robin had heard nothing from Lark, and he was desperate to know what had happened. While he kneaded bread, he worried that the king had refused to let her marry him. He also feared she had decided his jokes weren't any good and had changed her mind about loving him.

Golly, standing at his elbow, talked about going to Ooth Town for their honeymoon to see the roundest clock in Biddle. Then she left to try on her wedding dress.

Someone in the bakery said the word *princess*.

Robin's head shot up. He stopped kneading.

"What seems to be the princess's troublicament?" Nat asked the schoolteacher.

"She never stops crying. Give me six scones."

Oh, no! Robin tried not to shout. "Why is she crying?"

"I'm not sure, but the king is going to marry her off to the first person who makes her laugh." The schoolteacher didn't know the person had to be a prince. "The contest is being held in the tournament arena."

Robin knocked over the kneading table and rushed out of the bakery. He had to think.

Back inside, Matt said, "The lad is flipliddified and madaddlated."

Robin paced up and down in the bakery yard. When the schoolteacher had said that Lark was weeping, Robin had thought it meant the king had refused to let them marry. And then, for one glorious moment, when the schoolteacher had described the contest, he'd thought it was for him, that it was Lark's way of bringing them together. But if it was, then why was she crying?

Something terrible must have happened.

He started striding to the castle. He'd tell the guards he wanted to compete in the contest, so they'd let him in. He had to find out what was going on, although he wouldn't be able to compete. He was much too upset to make up jokes.

But the Royal Drawbridge Guard wouldn't let him pass. The guard didn't even let him say what he was there for.

Robin was beside himself. He'd have to marry Golly, or he'd have to run away, far from Lark. Either way, he'd lose his love. On his way home, he broke down and cried.

Golly thought a weeping Robin was the funniest thing she'd ever seen. Jake gave her towels to dry off the dough as Robin kneaded it. She wiped and laughed for an hour or two. Then she went back to the Sleep In, to monogram an extra dozen handkerchiefs for her trousseau.

Through his tears Robin watched her go. He wished Golly were a princess and that Lark were an innkeeper's daughter. He wished the guard had let him in. He wished Lark were here right this second. He wished.

Nine

Late that night the fairy Ethelinda flew over Biddle. She'd been flying for seven years, ever since she'd left the court of Anura, the fairy queen. Anura had scolded her for not giving a single reward or punishment to a human in centuries. Ethelinda had explained that she was afraid to because she'd bungled it the last time.

"Conquer your fear!" Anura had commanded. "Mingle with humans. Reward and punish. Do not disobey me!"

Ethelinda hadn't obeyed, but she hadn't disobeyed either. She'd just stayed in the air. But now she had to land. Seven years of flying were too much, even for a fairy. She was exhausted. She looked for a secluded spot where humans were unlikely to come. Ah. There.

She landed in a clearing in Snoakes Forest and stretched out under a pine tree, where she fell fast asleep.

The next morning, Jake packed a breakfast for Nat and sent him off early to chop wood. There was a lot to do today, and he wanted his two smart sons there to help him. He had to bake the usual quantities of bread, muffins, and scones, and he had to make the wedding cake for tomorrow.

Nat entered Snoakes Forest and went straight to the clearing where Ethelinda lay sleeping.

His footsteps woke her. She jumped up and took the shape of an old woman.

She hoped whoever was coming wouldn't do anything that required a reward or a punishment.

Nat entered the clearing. Ethelinda frowned at his basket, hoping he didn't have food in there. "Good day," she said in a voice that wavered.

"Good day." Nat smiled and bowed. He opened the basket and took out a jug of blackberry juice, three hard-boiled partridge eggs, and two fig-and-almond scones.

The dreaded meal! Ethelinda thought. The fairy rules were very clear. She had to ask the human to share. If he did share, she had to reward him. If he did not, she had to punish him.

"Kind sir," she said, "would you share your victuals with me?"

Nat knew Jake's rule. "No, Mistress. I am enormvastically sorry, but our family doesn't give our edibles or sip-pables to anyone."

She had to punish him! "So be it," she said. So be what? What should she do? She was shaking like a leaf.

Nat ate his breakfast.

Ethelinda thought of making him choke on a bone. But eggs and scones don't have bones. She didn't want to make snakes and insects come out of his mouth, because that hadn't been a great success the last time.

Nat patted his mouth with his napkin and stood up. "Please excusition me. Time to get to work." He picked up his ax and went to an oak tree.

She got it! She waved her wand, which was invisible because of her disguise.

Nat swung the ax. It slammed into the air six inches from the tree and stopped. It wouldn't go an inch closer no matter how hard he pushed.

"Huh? What—" He swung again. The ax stopped again.

He examined the ax. The blade was as sharpcuttable as ever. Something was protecting the tree. He reached out, expecting the something to stop his hand. But nothing did. He swung again. The ax slammed into the air and stopped again.

He frowned at the old lady. Did she cause this?

But she was leaning back against an elm tree with her eyes closed. Besides, what could she have done?

It must have been that tree. He went to a pine tree and swung the ax. It stopped six inches from the bark.

He ran from tree to tree, trying to chop down one after another. But he couldn't, not a single one. He screamed, not an invented word, not a word at all, only a scream. He ran out of the clearing, still screaming.

Ethelinda resumed her fairy shape. She'd done it. Anura should be satisfied. Ethelinda flapped her wings—and barely got off the ground. She was still exhausted. She landed in a heap and stayed there.

When Nat got home from the forest, he was muttering to himself and swinging the ax wildly. Matt feared that he might have become as goofdoltish as Robin, and Jake agreed. They pinned Nat to the ground and took the ax.

Robin didn't notice. Tomorrow was the wedding. It would be the end of everything.

Matt packed a brunch. If Nat couldn't cut down a tree, he, Matt, certainly would be able to. Hadn't he been axchopperizing trees since he was seven years old? He set off while Jake mixed batter for three dozen muffin tins.

As soon as Ethelinda heard Matt coming, she turned herself back into the old lady. When he too refused to share his meal, she punished him exactly as she'd punished Nat.

Jake became seriously worried when Matt returned in the same state as Nat. Jake thought,

> Now all my sons have lost their
>   wits,
> And Nat and Matt are having
>   conniptions.

Jake couldn't go to the forest himself. He had twenty-seven loaves of bread in the oven plus all those muffins and no sane son to watch them. Robin would have to go. Jake packed a lunch and put the ax in Robin's hand. He watched Robin go and then got to work on the wedding cake.

Ethelinda was delighted to see Robin. This punishment was terrific. She couldn't wait to use it again.

Robin put down his basket. It didn't occur to him to eat. He wasn't thinking at all. His mind was just bleating *Lark! Lark!* again and again. He staggered to a maple tree and raised his ax.

"Wait, kind sir!" Ethelinda went to him and stopped his hand. "Don't you want your lunch?"

What was she saying? Something about his lunch? He mumbled, "Don't want it."

"Oh, kind sir, may I have some?"

Lark! Lark! He raised the ax again.

"Kind sir!" Ethelinda shrieked. She

grabbed the ax and wrestled it away from Robin. She faced him, panting. "May I eat some of your lunch?"

Lark! Lark! "Go ahead."

Go ahead?

Oh no! She handed the ax back to him. Now she had to reward him, which was where she'd made her biggest mistake the last time.

She opened his basket and took out a wedge of Snetter cheese and a poppyseed roll. What could she give him? She couldn't think of a single foolproof reward.

Robin began to chop down the maple.

Then Ethelinda remembered a reward the fairy queen, Anura, had told her about. It was a bit odd, but Anura said she'd used it hundreds of times and it had always worked.

Robin raised the ax again. One more

chop and the maple would go over.

Ethelinda raised her invisible wand.

Robin swung the ax.

Ethelinda waved the wand.

The tree went over.

Honk! A golden goose stood on the stump, ruffling her golden feathers.

"HONK!"

Ten

Robin didn't notice the goose. He began to hack off the maple's branches.

"Oh," Ethelinda said, "what a beautiful golden goose!"

Robin felt a stab of exasperation. "You can have her."

Ethelinda stared in shock at him. And saw how unhappy he looked. "Why, what's the trouble, kind sir?"

He shook his head and chopped the maple into logs.

She made her voice sympathetic and comforting. "You can tell me. I'll understand."

The sweetness of her voice reached him. He looked up. Ethelinda made her expression kindly and patient.

He found himself talking. "I love Princess Lark and I hate . . ." He told the whole story. It was a relief to tell someone.

Ethelinda wasn't sure what good the goose would do, but she had faith in Anura. "Pick up the goose," she said. "Take her to the castle."

"I won't be able to get past the guards." He didn't move.

"Pick up the goose!" Ethelinda bellowed.

He began to pick up the logs.

"With that goose, no one will stop you." Ethelinda didn't know if this was true, but she'd make it true.

He dropped the logs and picked up the goose.

Honk!

He didn't believe no one would stop him, but he'd try anyway.

Ethelinda asked where he was going, just to make sure.

"To the princess."

At last. "The goose is sticky, so you may need these words: *Loose, goose.* Don't forget them."

The goose was sticky? What did that mean? Robin picked up a fallen leaf and touched it to the goose's feathers. It stuck. He said, "Loose, goose." The leaf fluttered to the ground.

Hmm. He had an idea. He left the clearing, walking fast.

Ethelinda brushed grass off her skirts. She felt rested, refreshed. She hurried after Robin. "I'll come too, kind sir. I may be able to help if anything goes wrong."

When he got near the Sleep In, Robin slowed to a saunter. If Golly didn't see him, he'd bang on the door. If he had to, he'd shove the goose up against her.

Upstairs in the inn, Golly was embroidering and looking out the window. Huh! she thought. There was Robin, with a goose in his arms and an old woman at his side. Golly squinted. What a fine golden goose. She frowned. Why wasn't he bringing the goose to her?

Because he was her dim-witted dearie. She laughed. "Look!"

Holly and Molly came to the window.

"We could cook the goose and share the feathers," Golly said.

The three of them ran downstairs and crowded out of the inn. Robin pretended not to see them and hurried off again.

"Dearie," Golly called, laughing. "Wait for me."

He kept going. They ran after him. Golly reached him first. She grabbed the goose's tail and pulled.

Honk!

Golly laughed. "Dearie!"

Robin heard her, but he didn't turn around. He hoped Holly and Molly would touch the goose too, and he hoped they'd stick too. Otherwise Golly had better look very funny, because she was all he'd have to make Lark laugh.

The goose pecked Golly's arm.

Yow! Golly tried to let go, but she couldn't. She stopped laughing. She was beginning to be annoyed.

Molly had almost reached the goose.

Golly yelled, "Don't touch the—"

"What?" Molly grasped Golly's elbow and didn't touch the goose.

"I'm stuck. Pull me off."

Molly pulled.

Honk!

But Golly stayed stuck.

"Help me, Holly!" Molly called, and held out her hand. "Pull!"

Holly took the hand and pulled.

Honk!

But Golly stayed stuck.

The three of them trotted after the goose. In a few minutes, Molly got tired. "I'm going home." She tried to let go of Golly's elbow. She yanked and tugged.

Honk!

She was stuck.

Holly tried to let go of Molly's hand, but she was stuck too.

71

Eleven

Hmm . . . Robin thought, glancing back. Whoever touches the goose becomes sticky. And the next person and the next become sticky too! He wondered how long a chain he could make. They did look funny, the three of them.

Golly was angry. "Dearie, stop this instant!"

Ethelinda didn't care a bit for Golly. Now *there* was a human who could use punishing.

Robin saw a mule and wagon in the distance, coming back from Biddle Castle.

It was the Snettering-on-Snoakes
chandler. He wondered where Robin was
going with that goose and why Golly,
Holly, and Molly were traipsing after
him. And who was the old lady?

"Whoa, Jenny," he called to his mule.

Holly, Molly, and Golly yelled to the
chandler to set them loose. When he
understood what they wanted, he tied a
rope to Jenny's harness and threw the
rope over Holly.

Oh, no! Robin thought. The goose
can't be stronger than a mule.

"Pull, Jenny. Pull."

Jenny tried, but she couldn't. She got
pulled instead.

The goose *is* stronger! Robin thought.

The chandler tried to jump down from
his cart to see what was wrong, but he
couldn't. He was stuck to his bench.

Robin glanced back and almost

laughed. The beginning of a joke came to him. Why does a king always seem glum? But he was still too upset to think of the punch line.

The chandler and his cart and mule followed Robin and the golden goose. Holly and Molly kept hollering that Jenny should try harder. Golly kept screaming at Robin to stop, to listen, to behave himself . . . dearie.

The Royal Drawbridge Guard saw a strange parade, heading for Biddle Castle. He frowned. There was the chandler. But the chandler had left only a little while ago. Who were the others with him?

The chandler looked flustered. Could be trouble. The guard got his pike ready.

They came closer. The guard wondered why the chandler and his mule and wagon and three wenches were following a lad with a golden goose. Why were the wenches shouting? Why did the mule look so confused? And who was the old lady?

Then the guard understood. The lad was really a prince! A contestant! The guard started laughing and put down his pike. This was so funny. It was sure to win. He bowed as Robin approached.

Robin thought, He's letting me in! The old lady is right! Maybe he'd like to come along too. He called, "Help yourself to a feather."

The guard lunged at the goose.

Honk!

The guard was stuck.

Robin was going by the Royal Kitchen Door just as the Royal Third Assistant Cook stepped outside.

My, the cook thought, that's a fine pair of goose feet, perfect for pickling. He reached out and grabbed the goose's right foot.

Honk!

In the Royal Tournament Arena Lark wept on. So far seventy-five princes had tried to make her laugh. The king and the Royal Nobles were merrier than ever before. But Lark's eyes hurt from crying so much. Two Royal Laundresses worked day and night to keep her in fresh hankies.

Right now a prince was saying "Fif-fifferall" over and over. At first no one had laughed, but after a few minutes a Royal Baroness had begun to giggle, and then the Royal Chief Councillor had joined in, and soon everyone was laughing heartily.

Except Lark, of course.

A commotion at the arena's entrance drowned out the prince. Heads turned. Lark didn't look up.

Robin, Holly, Molly, Golly, the Royal Drawbridge Guard, and the Royal Third Assistant Cook jogged into the arena. Behind them, the chandler, Jenny, and the cart clattered along. Ethelinda skipped and leaped and waved her arms in the air, to add to the silliness.

Robin saw Lark. There she was. Weeping! Her sweet face was unutterably sad. She was wiping her eyes and staring at her lap. She hadn't even seen him.

He broke into a run. *Lark! Oh, Lark!*

Twelve

King Harrumphrey and the courtiers saw the goose parade and roared with laughter. Even the prince saying "Fif-fifferall" laughed. The Earl of Pildenue fell out of his seat, laughing. Dame Cloris woke up and started laughing. King Harrumphrey rocked back and forth on his throne.

Lark wept and never looked up. Where was her love now? Did he miss her?

Robin moaned. Whatever had happened to Lark must have been—must still be—awful. He began to cry in sympathy.

Under the laughter and the shrieks, Lark heard a new sound. She closed her eyes to hear better. Someone else was weeping.

Robin ran across the arena. He shouted, "Oh, Lark! Oh, my love! Oh, don't cry!"

She opened her eyes. Robin? Here? Yes! She smiled rapturously at him. Just at him—because she didn't notice the guard, the cook, Ethelinda, Golly, Molly, Holly, the chandler, Jenny, the cart, or the goose.

She's smiling! Robin thought. He smiled back at her through his tears.

Lark jumped up, knocking over her outdoor throne. Then she saw the spectacle behind Robin. They were so funny! She ran down the arena steps, laughing as she ran.

Ethelinda laughed too. Giving a

successful reward was its own reward.

Robin thought of the punch line for the joke about why a king seems glum. He laughed. His laughter shook the goose.

Honk!

Golly shrieked, "Dearie! Get away from that princess."

Robin said, "Loose, goose."

Holly, Molly, Golly, the chandler, the mule, the cart, the Royal Drawbridge Guard, and the Royal Third Assistant Cook were released from their hold on the goose and each other.

Royal Nobles poured onto the field. They surrounded Robin and bowed to him and shouted, "Congratulations!" Ethelinda stood at the edge of the crowd. She was sure she'd never have trouble with rewards again, now that she'd found the goose.

"Harrumph."

The crowd parted for King Harrum-phrey.

He was delighted to see Larkie laughing again. And this young prince had done it cleverly. Dressing like a commoner—very smart. He'd make a fine son-in-law. "We are pleased to make your harrumphance, Your Highness." He put his arm around Robin's shoulder. "What kingdom do you harrumph from?"

Highness? Kingdom? Who did the king think he was? Robin knelt. "I live in Snettering-on-Snoakes, Sire. I'm Robin, the baker's son."

He *is* a commoner! the king thought. He's that blasted baker's son.

"I want to marry him," Lark said.

King Harrumphrey wanted to throw him into the Royal Dungeon. But he couldn't, not with Larkie smiling at the boy in that demented way.

Golly opened her mouth to say that she was marrying Robin.

"Son," the king said, "only a prince could win the harrumph."

Golly shut her mouth.

Robin thought, So that's why Lark was weeping. He thought of weeping again himself, but he couldn't stop smiling at her.

King Harrumphrey turned to his daughter. "You don't want to harrumphy him, honeyharrumph. We'll give him a harrumphdred golden coins instead."

Ethelinda was furious. She hated a snob. Couldn't the king tell what a fine lad Robin was?

"No, Father. He doesn't want a gift."

"A harrumphdred golden coins and a golden cage for that golden harrumph."

"No thank you, Your Majesty."

"Father, I'm going to cry again."

"Don't harrumph. We hate it when you harrumph. Let us think." He couldn't let her marry a commoner. What would his Royal Forebears have done? Well, King Humphrey IV would have devised a test. What kind of test? Hmm . . .

"We will consent to the harrumphage," he said, "if the lad can pass three harrumphs. For the first harrumph he must find someone who can drink a whole cellar full of harrumph." He saw Lark's expression. "Very fine harrumph. Only the best."

Golly laughed. Her dearie would never pass the test.

Who could drink so much? Robin wondered. And what's harrumph? Beet juice? Bat's milk?

I can do it, Ethelinda thought. I can drink anything.

"The second harrumph is to find someone who can eat a hill of harrumphs as
tall as our Royal Glass Hill."

Now what's harrumph? Robin thought.
Skunk sausages?

"And the third harrumph . . ." The
king paused for effect. ". . . is to come
to Biddle Castle on a ship that harrumphs on land or water."

Lark frowned. "What?"

"A harrumph that sails on land or harrumph." No commoner can pass these
tests, King Harrumphrey thought. But
if this upstart does, we'll dream up three
more tests, and then three more. As
many as it takes.

Thirteen

The third test might be hard, Ethelinda thought.

Robin couldn't imagine how he'd pass any of them. He was going to lose Lark all over again.

"The tests are impossible," Lark wailed.

"Sweetie, this harrumph has already made you laugh, and you and we thought that was imharrumphible."

But that was because he's my love, she thought. And because he's funnier than anyone else.

Robin remembered that the old lady had said she might be able to help him some more. He turned her way, and she winked at him—although she still wasn't sure about the last test.

Robin began to have a suspicion about her. "I'll try," he told the king. He bowed. "Farewell." Farewell, my love.

"Farewell." Lark smiled bravely.

Robin picked up the goose and started out of the arena. Ethelinda walked at his side. Golly began to go with them, but the fairy waved her invisible wand.

Golly's feet wouldn't move, no matter how hard she tried. "Dearie, I want to come with you."

He kept walking.

"Get back here and help me, dearie."

He walked faster.

When they were out of sight of the castle, Robin said, "You're a fairy, aren't you?"

Smart human! Ethelinda resumed her normal form.

Honk!

Robin staggered back. She was gigantic! And those wings! Pink, fleshy, and vast.

He thought it might be a good idea to bow, so he did. "Will you help me?"

She turned herself into a hungry-and-thirsty-looking beggar. "This is the right shape for the first two tests, don't you think?"

He nodded. They waited a half hour so it would seem as if he had spent some time searching for someone. Then they started back to the tournament arena.

Meanwhile, King Harrumphrey was annoyed because he'd used up seven hundred kegs of cider flooding the basement of the Royal Museum of Quest Souvenirs. Worse, he had no idea how he was going to un-flood it when Robin's person failed to drink it dry.

But in case whoever it was succeeded,

the king had ordered the Royal Kitchen to cook thousands of meatballs for the second test. Most likely everybody at the castle was going to be eating meatballs till meatballs came out of their eyeballs.

Lark felt a little hope when she saw the beggar, who was as skinny as one of the goose's legs. His cracked and chapped tongue hung out, for certain the driest tongue in Biddle. King Harrumphrey started to worry.

Holly, Molly, the chandler, the guard, and the cook had left. Golly had stayed, although the spell on her feet had worn off.

At the museum a Royal Servant opened the trapdoor to the cellar. Cider lapped against the ceiling. Robin put the goose down and stood next to Lark to watch.

"TILL MEATBALLS CAME OUT OF THEIR EYEBALLS."

Ethelinda used her fairy powers to discover if anything was in the cellar besides cider. Seventeen rats, drinking and swimming. She made them vanish. She didn't want their whiskers anywhere near her mouth, and she didn't want King Harrumphrey to claim that she'd had help drinking a single sip.

The servant handed her a ladle.

A ladle! It would take years with a ladle. Ethelinda waved it aside and lowered her head into the cellar.

She began to drink. The first seventy gallons were delicious, but after that she wished someone had thought to add cinnamon. When a hundred kegs were gone, she could no longer reach low enough to drink. The servant went for a ladder.

While they waited, Ethelinda said, "Thank you, Sire. I would have perished of thirst if not for you. I only hope there's enough here to satisfy me."

King Harrumphrey nodded and tried to look gracious. Lark and Robin held hands while he whispered jokes into her ear. Her favorite was Why are elves delicious? She thought the answer was hysterical: Because they're brownies.

Golly glared at Lark, Robin, the goose, and the beggar. She swore to give that beggar a kick if he ever showed up at her inn.

The king thought up two additional tests, in case he needed them. He'd make Robin find someone who could play twenty musical instruments at once and someone who could go up the Royal Grand Staircase on his head.

The servant returned with a ladder. Ethelinda descended two rungs and drank.

In an hour the cellar was dry. King Harrumphrey inspected it carefully, hoping against hope that he'd find at least a drop of cider, but he didn't.

It took Ethelinda one and a half hours to finish the meatballs. When she was done, she bowed to the king and burped.

King Harrumphrey said, "Robin, you must harrumph back here in two hours with a harrumph that can sail on land or sea."

Lark said, "You didn't say there was a time limit."

"Two harrumphs and no longer. By Royal Harrumph!"

Fourteen

In a field beyond the castle, Robin patted the goose and waited for Ethelinda to create the ship. Instead, she sat on the ground and put her head in her hands.

He cleared his throat uneasily. "Is there a problem?"

"I'm thinking." She could make a beautiful ship, one that could weather any storm. But on shore it wouldn't budge. She could make a wonderful carriage that would go anywhere on land, even without a road. But in water it would sink.

Robin said, "What if the sails turn into

wings when the boat reaches the shore?"

"Then the king would say it's a bird on land and not a boat."

The minutes ticked by. An hour passed. The sky began to get dark.

An hour and a half passed. The stars came out.

Maybe the lad was on the right track with the wings idea, Ethelinda thought.

Fifteen more minutes passed.

What if she filled the hold with wings? Not birds, just wings. When the ship was on land, the wings would fly up against the ceiling of the hold and lift the ship off the ground.

That was the way to do it. She waved her wand.

Robin gasped. The boat was beautiful, painted yellow with blue trim. The sails were blindingly white. If it could move on land, it would pass the test.

But King Harrumphrey probably still

wouldn't let him marry Lark. The king would think of more and more tests, until the fairy got sick of tests and left him.

I have to think of a way to make this the last one, Robin thought. He stared at the ship. It needed something, something to show what kind of ship it was. It needed a pennant.

A pennant! That was it.

"Is there any empty land far from here where I could be prince?" he asked.

Ethelinda thought for a moment. "You could be Prince of the Briny Isles. This ship will get you there in seven years. You'll starve to death, though, unless you like anchovies."

"That doesn't matter." If he actually had to go there, his idea would have failed. "Would you make a pennant that says 'Prince Robin of the Briny Isles'?"

She did, and she dressed him as a

prince, in a red satin robe and a doublet with diamond buttons. On his head she placed a silver crown set with rubies.

They mounted a plank onto the ship. It set sail across the field. The boat was a glorious sight, skimming a foot above the ground, its sails bellying out in the breeze.

When the boat reached the castle, it descended into the moat, to prove that it could sail on water too. Then it rose again and stopped a few yards from Lark, the king, and Golly, who were standing near the castle drawbridge. Ethelinda, disguised as a nobleman, threw a ladder over the side. Robin and the nobleman climbed down and bowed. The goose remained on deck, strutting up and down and honking.

Lark curtsied and said, "Your Highness."

King Harrumphrey scowled. The lad

looked better, but a baker's son in prince's clothing was still a baker's son.

Golly gasped. Robin had passed every test. He was going to marry the princess! How dared he? She screamed, "Dearie, I wouldn't marry you if you were the stupidest lad in Biddle. You led me—"

"Be silent," Robin said. "I command it."

Golly was so surprised, she fell silent.

He sounds princely, King Harrumphrey thought, but still . . .

Ethelinda said, "I am the Duke of Halibutia and the envoy of the King of the Briny Isles. He sent me here to find an heir worthy to rule after his death, and I have found him. Prince Robin has more natural royalty than anyone I've ever encountered."

"Sire," Robin said, "I have passed your tests. Give me your daughter's hand in marriage."

"Do, Father. Please."

Robin continued. "Then we shall depart for my kingdom, which is seven years' sailing from here." He held his breath, hoping.

King Harrumphrey frowned. Since the envoy—a duke!—had chosen Robin, then the lad had truly become a prince. But seven years! Even if they turned around and came back as soon as they got there, the king still wouldn't see his Larkie for fourteen years.

He couldn't live for fourteen years without the sight of her. "Harrumph. Er, we admit that you are a prince, but can't you stay here? Can't those Briny Harrumphs do without you?"

"If I stay here, I'll just be a baker's son."

"Father . . ."

King Harrumphrey looked at his

daughter. She was half smiling. He knew what would turn that smile into a laugh. And he knew what would turn it into a frown and tears.

There had been enough tears. "No, you will not be a baker's harrumph. You will be a Harrumph Prince of Biddle."

Lark and Robin hugged each other. They danced across the Royal Drawbridge and back again.

Robin was so happy, he decided to try out a joke on King Harrumphrey. He said, "Why does a king always seem glum?"

King Harrumphrey frowned. What was the fellow talking about?

Lark was thrilled. Now Father would see what Robin was really like. "Why?" she said.

"Because he's . . ." Robin sighed dramatically. ". . . a sire."

The king stared. Then he got it. A sire. A sigh-er! He started laughing. "Har har harrumph." It was the funniest joke he'd ever heard. "A harrumph-er!" This commoner-turned-prince would liven up the castle. "Har harrumph har. Harrumph har har."

Lark preferred the yardstick-ruler joke. But if Father loved this one, that was all that mattered.

Epilogue

Jake was as opposed to the match between Robin and Lark as King Harrumphrey had been. He said,

> *"I forbid the marriage with*
> *Princess Lark.*
> *I would rather see the boy wed a*
> *barracuda."*

King Harrumphrey offered to elevate Jake to the rank of earl and to knight Nat and Matt, who had finally recovered from Ethelinda's spell.

The three of them refused to become

nobles. However, Jake agreed to the wedding when the king named him Royal Chief Poet and named Nat and Matt Royal Co-Chief Dictionarians in charge of adding new words to Biddlish.

Robin and Lark were married within a week, and the whole population of Snettering-on-Snoakes was invited, even though every one of them was a commoner.

King Harrumphrey performed the wedding ceremony, although Lark and Robin weren't sure if the harrumphiage they were entering into was their marriage or their carriage.

Dame Cloris snored straight through the king's speech. Golly stayed awake. She sat next to the chandler and decided he was the man for her. If she couldn't boss him around, she'd boss Jenny the mule.

After the ceremony Robin told a joke:

"Why is a horse like a wedding?"

He waited, but not one of the guests could think of the answer, so he told them, "They both need a groom."

Lark laughed and laughed. She felt so proud of Robin, the funniest prince in Biddle history.

Jake wasn't sure he got the joke. His own Horsteed had never had a groom in his life. But he smiled and waited for the laughter to subside, so he could recite a poem to Robin.

"I thought to maiden Golly you'd
be wed,
But you married Princess Lark in
place of her."

Robin and Lark thanked Ethelinda over and over for her help. Their gratitude went a long way toward restoring her confidence, and she was certain she'd never make another mistake.

The party after the ceremony was held on the bank of Snoakes Stream. Robin and Lark waded right in and pulled courtiers and commoners in after them for a Royal Splashfest. The golden goose waddled in too and splashed and honked at everybody. Lark was in heaven, splashing dukes and counts, and having them splash her right back.

And they all lived happily ever after.

Harrumph!

Honk!